Henry Helps
with
Dinner

written by Beth Bracken   illustrated by Ailie Busby

PICTURE WINDOW BOOKS
a capstone imprint

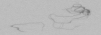

Henry Helps books are published by Picture Window Books
A Capstone Imprint
1710 Roe Crest Drive
North Mankato, Minnesota 56003
www.capstonepub.com

Library of Congress Cataloging-in-Publication Data
Bracken, Beth.
Henry helps with dinner / by Beth Bracken ; illustrated by Ailie Busby.
p. cm. -- (Henry helps)
ISBN 978-1-4048-6773-4 (library binding)
ISBN 978-1-4048-7675-0 (paperback)
[1. Helpfulness--Fiction.] I. Busby, Ailie, ill. II. Title. III. Series.

PZ7.B6989Hen 2011
[E]--dc22
2010050100

Graphic Designer: Russell Griesmer
Creative Director: Heather Kindseth
Production Specialist: Michelle Biedscheid

Printed in the United States of America in North Mankato, Minnesota.
062017
101578R

For Sam, the best helper I know. — BB

It's taco night!

Henry can't wait!

He loves taco night.

"I need your help, Henry!" Dad calls.

"Okay!" Henry says.

Before he helps Dad,
Henry washes his hands
and dries them carefully.

He watches Dad shred the cheese.

Then Henry carries the bowl to the table.

Henry puts one napkin at each place.

One, two, three.

Henry puts his sippy cup by his napkin.

He will have milk with his dinner.

Mom and Dad are having juice.

"Please rip up this lettuce," says Dad.

"Make the pieces nice and small."

Next, Henry smooshes an avocado

while Dad chops an onion.

"Time to eat!" says Dad.

"Dinner looks great!" says Mom.

"I helped!" says Henry.

Yum, yum!